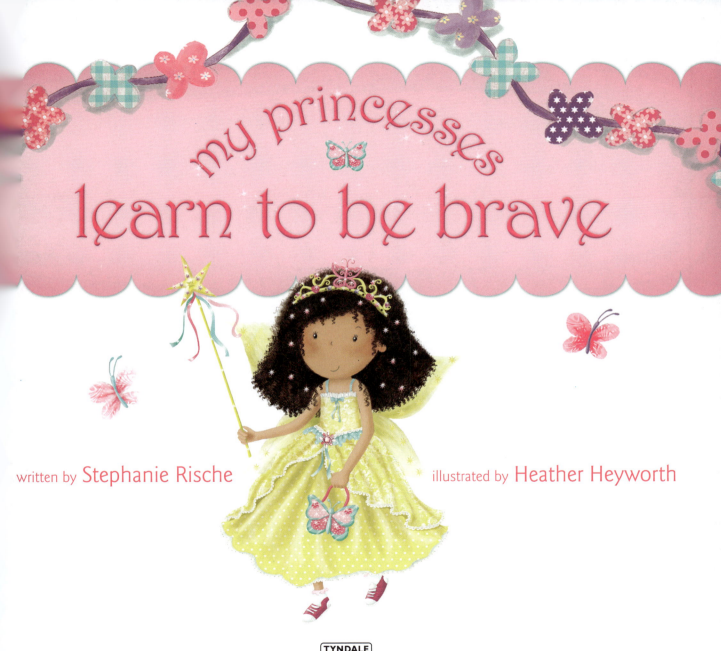

my princesses
learn to be brave

written by Stephanie Rische

illustrated by Heather Heyworth

TYNDALE KIDS

Tyndale House Publishers, Inc. | Carol Stream, IL

Visit Tyndale's website for kids at www.tyndale.com/kids.

TYNDALE is a registered trademark of Tyndale House Publishers, Inc. The Tyndale Kids logo is a trademark of Tyndale House Publishers, Inc.

My Princesses Learn to Be Brave

Copyright © 2014 Tyndale House Publishers, Inc.

Illustrations by Heather Heyworth. Copyright © by Tyndale House Publishers, Inc. All rights reserved.

Designed by Jacqueline L. Nuñez

Edited by Brittany Buczynski

Scripture quotations are taken from the *Holy Bible*, New Living Translation, copyright © 1996, 2004, 2007, 2013 by Tyndale House Foundation. Used by permission of Tyndale House Publishers, Inc.

Carol Stream, Illinois 60188. All rights reserved.

For manufacturing information regarding this product, please call 1-800-323-9400.

ISBN 978-1-4143-9661-3

Printed in China

20	19	18	17	16	15	14
7	6	5	4	3	2	1

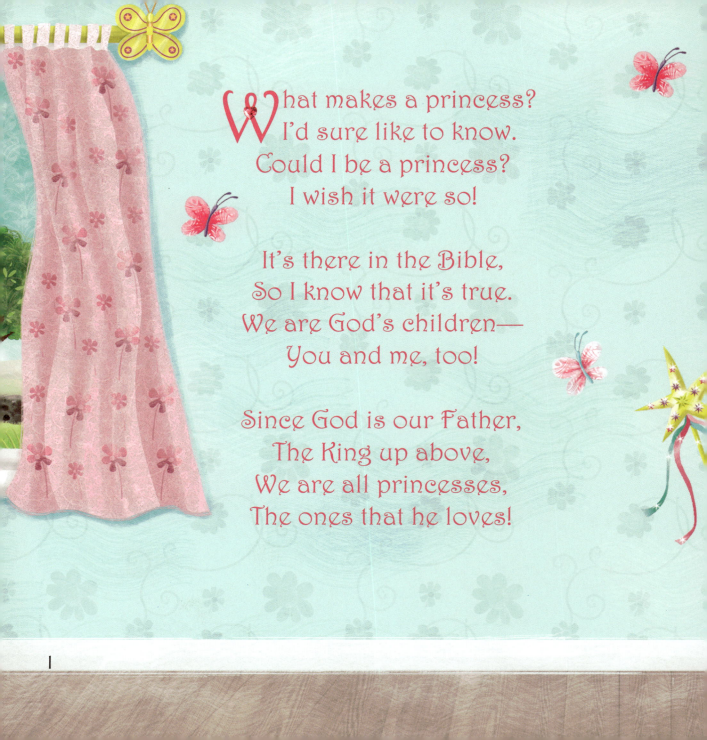

What makes a princess?
I'd sure like to know.
Could I be a princess?
I wish it were so!

It's there in the Bible,
So I know that it's true.
We are God's children—
You and me, too!

Since God is our Father,
The King up above,
We are all princesses,
The ones that he loves!

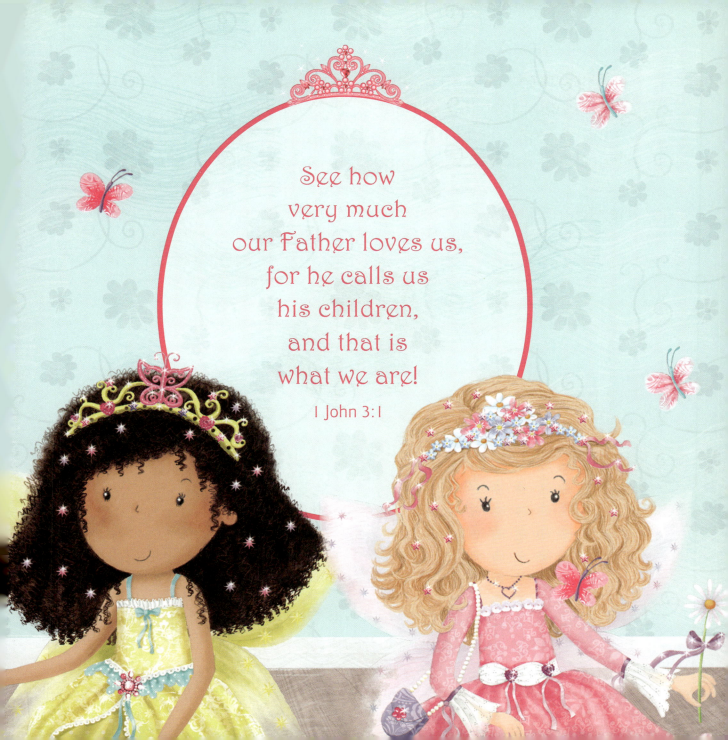

See how
very much
our Father loves us,
for he calls us
his children,
and that is
what we are!

1 John 3:1

Princess Grace straightened the crown on her head and stepped into her carriage. She was going to the castle today! It was a long trip. Once she got there, she would head straight to the steps and climb up to the tall tower.

Her friend Princess Hope would be waiting for her there!

Grace was so excited. Today Mom was taking her to the park! She and her friend Hope loved to play dress-up together and pretend they were

princesses. The playground was a perfect castle for them.

Soon Grace arrived at the park. She saw her friend Hope right away. "Greetings, Princess Hope," Grace said.

"How do you do, Princess Grace?" Hope asked.

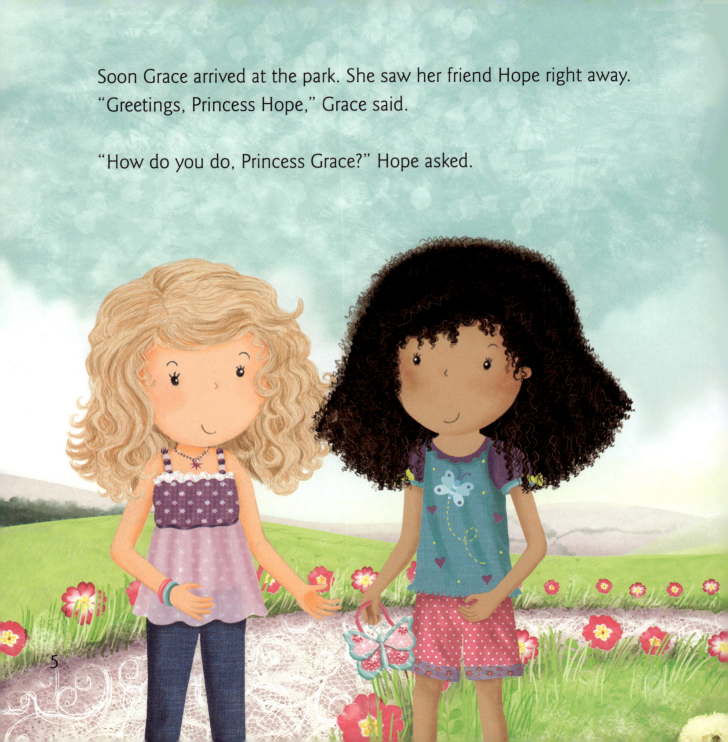

The two girls ran as fast as they could to their favorite slide—the tallest one in the park. They liked to pretend it was a tower in a castle.

They climbed up the steps. But just when they were almost to the top, they stopped.

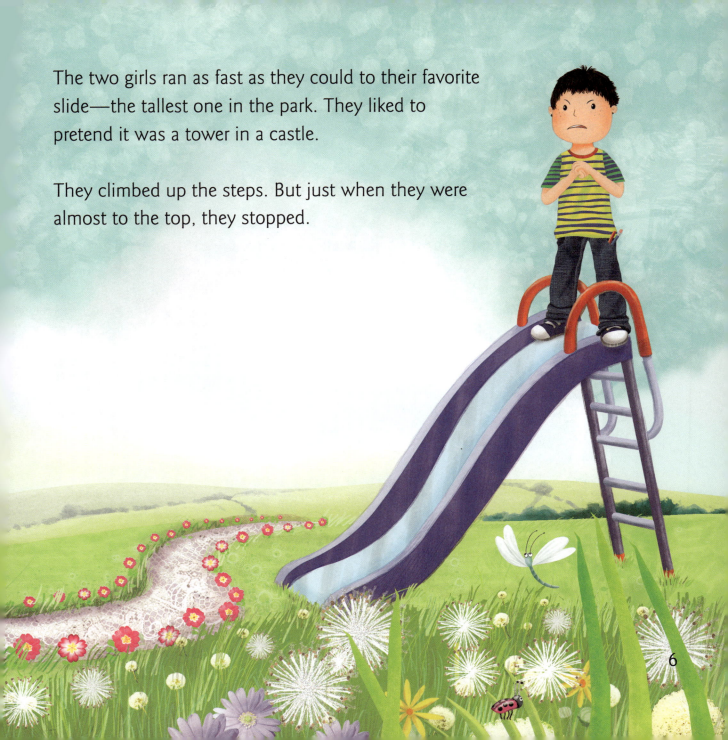

"Oh, no!" Grace said. "It's that mean bully again! He never lets us play on the slide."

"Let's try," Hope said. "Maybe he'll be nice to us today."

But as soon as the girls took one more step, the bully turned around and yelled at them.

"What are you doing on MY slide?" he shouted.

"We just want to play princesses up here," Grace said.

"No way," the boy said. **"There are NO GIRLS ALLOWED on my slide!"**

7

Grace and Hope turned around and went back down the steps.
They sat on the swings and tried to figure out what to do.

"Why is that boy always so mean to us?" Hope asked. She started
to cry.

9

"He's just a bully," Grace said. "Hey, that reminds me of a story I learned at church. It's from the Bible. Do you want to hear it?"

Hope nodded her head.

"A long time ago, there was a girl named Esther," Grace said. "She was just a regular girl. But then she married the king. That made her the new queen! Life was good at the castle . . . until one day when Queen Esther found out that her people were in trouble. A bad man named Haman made a new law. The law said that anyone in the land could hurt Esther's people."

"Queen Esther had a tough choice to make. Would she be really brave and help her people? Or would she stay quiet and let the bully keep being mean to everyone?"

"I bet she was brave!" Hope said.

"Yes," Grace said. "She was REALLY brave. First she asked for help—

from her family and from God. Then she went straight to the king to tell him what the bully was doing. She knew the king could have gotten very mad at her for going to him like that. But she did it anyway. Because Esther was so brave, her people were saved from the mean bully!"

"Wow! Do you think we could be that brave?" Hope asked. "Our bully is so scary."

"Wait, I have an idea!" Grace said.

Grace ran over to the edge of the playground and picked up a stick that was lying on the ground.

"What's that stick for?" Hope asked.

Grace pulled a scarf out of her purse and tied it to the end of the stick. "You mean this flag?" Grace said. "It's a present for our knight!"

Grace and Hope ran straight up the steps to the top of the tall slide.

Grace looked at the bully and smiled her bravest smile. "We need someone to be the mighty knight," she said.

"Would you like to play with us?" Hope asked the boy.

Grace held out the stick with the scarf tied to it. She waved it and said, "Every knight needs a special flag!"

The bully was so surprised. He looked at the girls and didn't say anything. Then he smiled, took the flag, and lifted it in the air. He was ready to play!

"Hello, princesses," the boy said. "My name is Lance, and I'm a mighty knight!" Holding his new flag, he helped the princesses step across into the castle tower.

And they all played happily ever after . . . until it was time to get in their carriage and head home for lunch.

Perhaps you were made queen
for just such a time as this.

—Esther 4:14

Stephanie Rische is a senior editor of nonfiction books at Tyndale House Publishers, as well as a freelance writer for various publications, including *Today's Christian Woman*, *Significant Living* magazine, Marriage Partnership, and her.meneutics. She and her husband, Daniel, live in the Chicago area, where they enjoy riding their bikes, making homemade ice cream, and swapping bad puns. She has several little princesses in her life, including her much-loved nieces.

Heather Heyworth lives and works in a sleepy Suffolk town in the United Kingdom. After graduating from Goldsmiths, University of London, with a diploma in art and design, she became creative manager at a design studio and then art editor at a greeting card publisher.

Her introduction to the world of children's books came when she illustrated, designed, and copublished her own licensed-character activity books. Since then, she has illustrated many titles, including picture books, board books, and educational books. She loves creating new characters, especially "butterfly princesses" who flutter around her imagination, scattering magical fairy dust as they go.